Edie
is ever so helpful!

Sophy Henn

Philomel Books

Hello!

My name is Edie.

I am **ever so** helpful.

In fact I think helping is
one of the things I am best at.

I start the day by helping everyone
wake up and get out of bed.

Mommy and Daddy find this rather tricky
so sometimes I have to help them
a little bit LOUDER.

When everyone is finally
up and zooming about
I like to help by getting
myself dressed.

And then I make breakfast.

Deeeeeeelicious!

After all that it's shoes on . . .

and off we pop!

At the shops I help Daddy find
everything we need.

And at the park I like to make sure that
everyone is having as much **fun** as possible.

When we get home I even help
put the shopping away.

After **all** that helping I can get a bit exhausted.
So I go and help the dog have a rest.

But soon enough I'm full of beans and
helping out **all over** the place.

Organizing Mommy's office . . .

and tidying up
with Daddy.

My brother is much, much littler than me,
so he needs lots of help . . .

with sharing . . .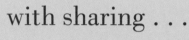

dressing up . . .

and knowing
what's what.

When they come to visit I love to help
Grandma with her makeup and
Grandpa with his hairstyles.

I mainly do this when they are asleep . . .

and they are mainly asleep so it
all works out terrrrrific!

I am **always** on the lookout for new
ways to be helpful. Like, maybe,
jazzing up the dog . . .

or making Daddy's shoes
a bit more snazzy.

. . . or even brightening the place up a bit!

Sometimes I have to remember
NOT to be quite so helpful.

But once I
have remembered
exactly how helpful
I should be . . .

I can get back to being my best
and helping everyone out again.

After all . . .

. . . I don't know **what** they'd do without me!

for Sarah Underhill who really has been ever so helpful

Also by Sophy Henn

Where Bear?

Pom Pom Panda Gets the Grumps

Pass It On

Philomel Books

an imprint of Penguin Random House LLC

375 Hudson Street, New York, NY 10014

Library of Congress Cataloging-in-Publication Data is available upon request.

Manufactured in China.

ISBN 9780399548062

1 3 5 7 9 10 8 6 4 2

Text set in Bodoni MT Std.